THE CHRISTMAS SONG

Chestnuts Roasting on an Open Fire

TO MY CHILDREN:

BENJAMIN, ARIANE, AND ELLIOT

—D.B.

The Christmas Song: Chestnuts Roasting on an Open Fire
Lyric and Music by Mel Tormé and Robert Wells © 1946 (Renewed) Edwin H. Morris & Company,
A Division of MPL Music Publishing, Inc., and Sony/ATV Tunes LLC
All Rights Reserved. Used by Permission.
Illustrations copyright © 2007 by Doris Barrette

Manufactured in China.
Library of Congress Cataloging-in-Publication Data is available.
ISBN-10: 0-06-072225-8 (trade bdg.) — ISBN-13: 978-0-06-072225-8 (trade bdg.)
ISBN-10: 0-06-072226-6 (lib.bdg.) — ISBN-13: 978-0-06-072226-5 (lib.bdg.)

Designed by Stephanie Bart-Horvath   1 2 3 4 5 6 7 8 9 10
❖
First Edition

THE CHRISTMAS SONG

Chestnuts Roasting on an Open Fire

BY MEL TORMÉ AND ROBERT WELLS
ILLUSTRATED BY DORIS BARRETTE

HARPERCOLLINSPUBLISHERS

CHESTNUTS ROASTING ON AN OPEN FIRE

JACK FROST NIPPING AT YOUR NOSE

YULETIDE CAROLS BEING SUNG BY A CHOIR

AND FOLKS DRESSED UP LIKE ESKIMOS.

EVERYBODY KNOWS A TURKEY AND SOME MISTLETOE

HELP TO MAKE THE SEASON BRIGHT.

Tiny tots with their eyes all aglow

WILL FIND IT HARD TO SLEEP TONIGHT.

THEY KNOW THAT SANTA'S ON HIS WAY

HE'S LOADED LOTS OF TOYS AND GOODIES
ON HIS SLEIGH

AND EVERY MOTHER'S CHILD IS GONNA SPY

To see if reindeer really know how to fly.

And so I'm offering this simple phrase
to kids from one to ninety-two.

ALTHOUGH IT'S BEEN SAID MANY TIMES,
MANY WAYS,

"Merry Christmas to you."